D0516213

If You See a Kitten

PEACHTREE
ATLANTA

For Joanna

Published by
PEACHTREE PUBLISHERS, LTD.
1700 Chattahoochee Avenue
Atlanta, Georgia 30318-2112

www.peachtree-online.com

First published in Great Britain in 2002 by the Penguin Group

Manufactured in Singapore

10 9 8 7 6 5 4 3 2 1
First Edition

Library of Congress Cataloging-in-Publication Data:

Butler, John.
If you see a kitten / written and illustrated by John Butler. – 1st ed.
p. cm.
Summary: Illustrations and brief text present appropriate responses to a variety of animals, from pudgy pigs to slithery snakes.

ISBN 1-56145-108-8

[1. Animals--Fiction.] I. Title.

PZ7.B97718If 2003
[E]--dc21 2002011552

If you see a
cuddly kitten ...

say,

"Ahhh!"

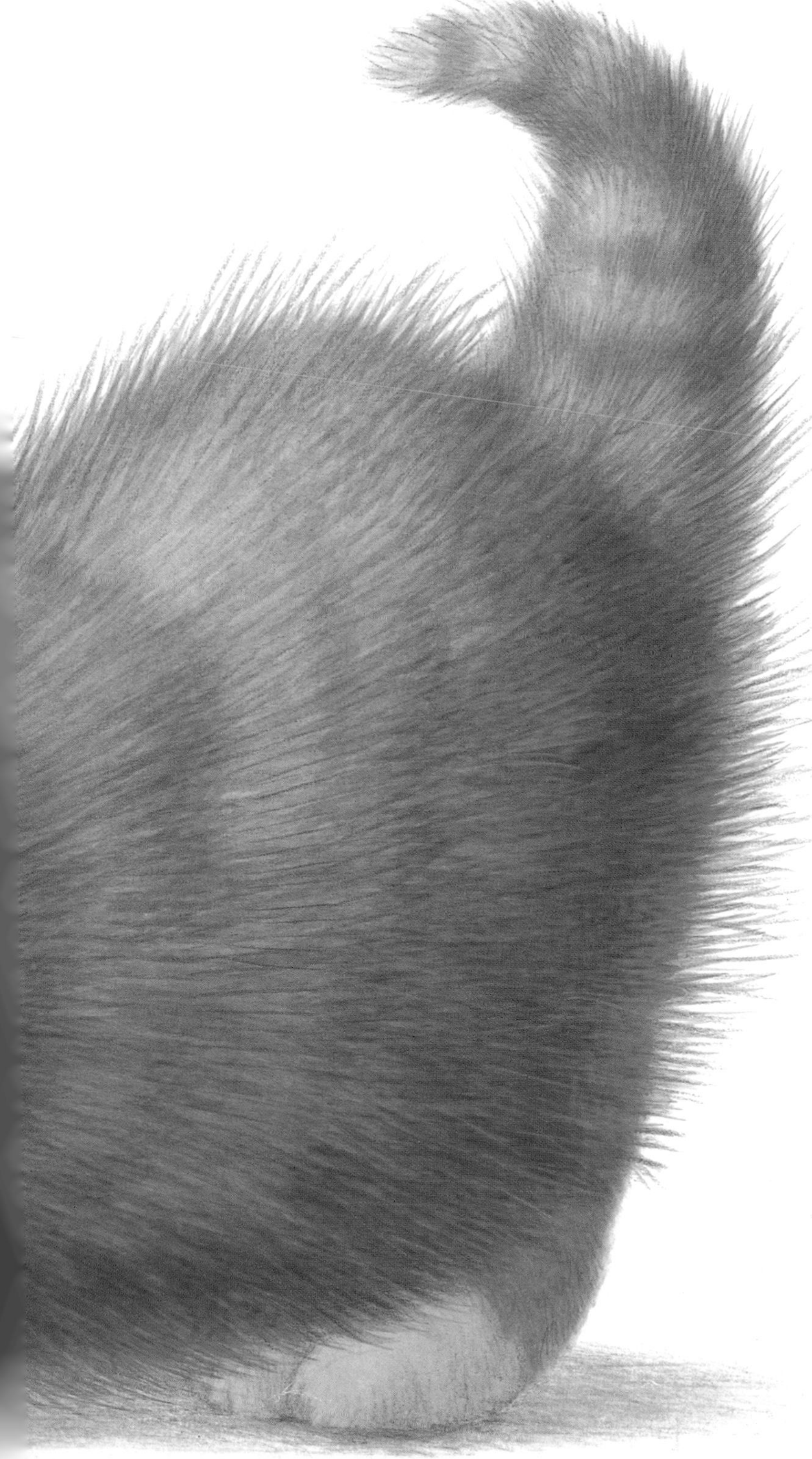

If you see
a pudgy pig ...

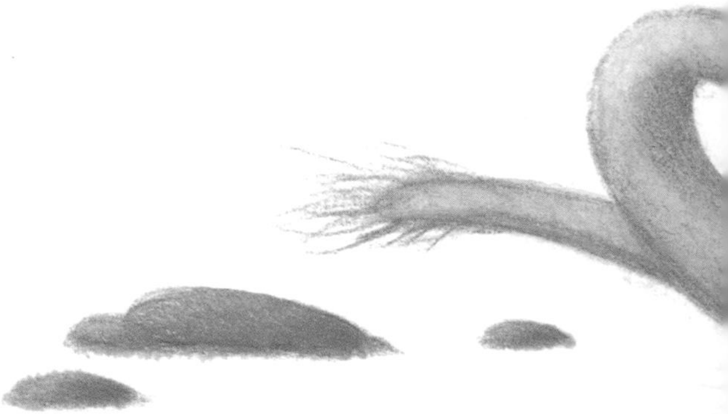

say,

*"Peee-
ew!"*

If you
see a dozing
dormouse ...

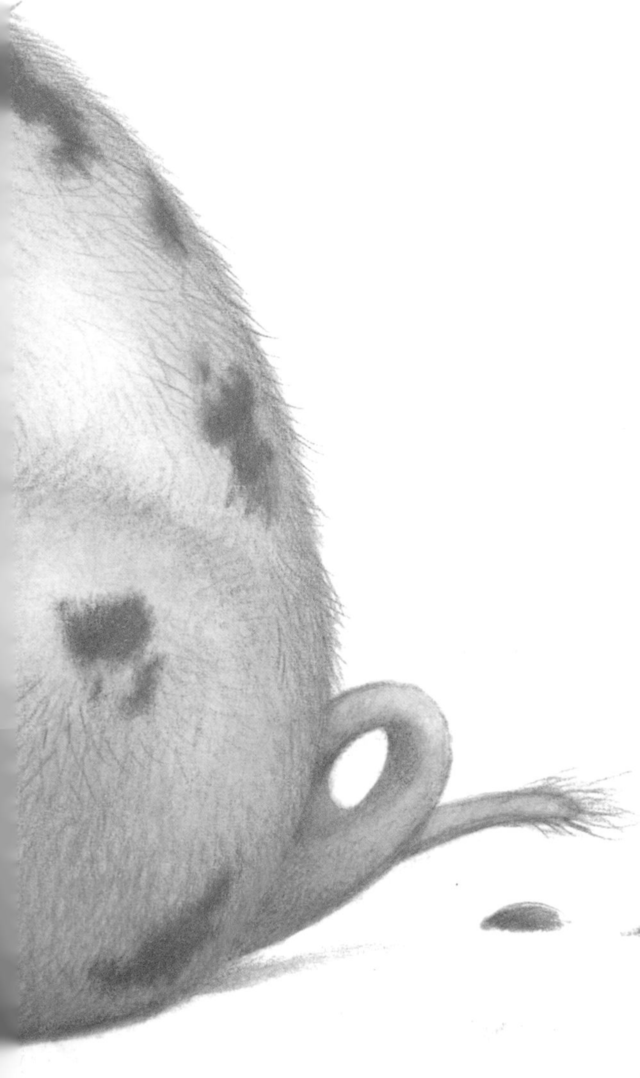

say,

"*Shhh!*"

If you see some
slimy slugs ...

say,

“Yuck!”

If you see
a pretty
peacock ...

say,

"Oooh!"

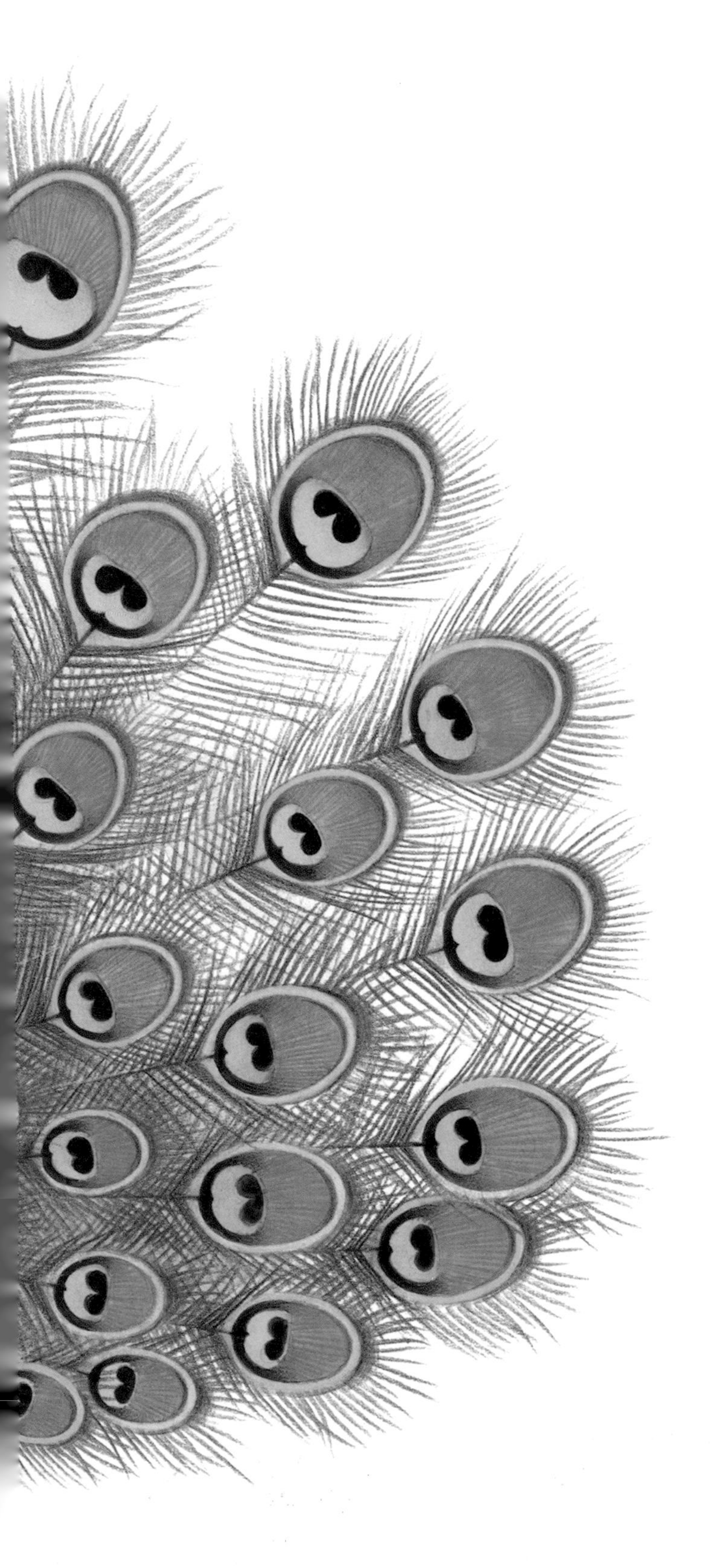

If you see
a slithery
snake ...

say,

“Yikes!”

If you see a
prickly porcupine ...

say,

"Ouch!"

If you see
an enormous
elephant ...

say,

“*Wow!*”

If you see a
spooky spider ...

say,

“Eeek!”

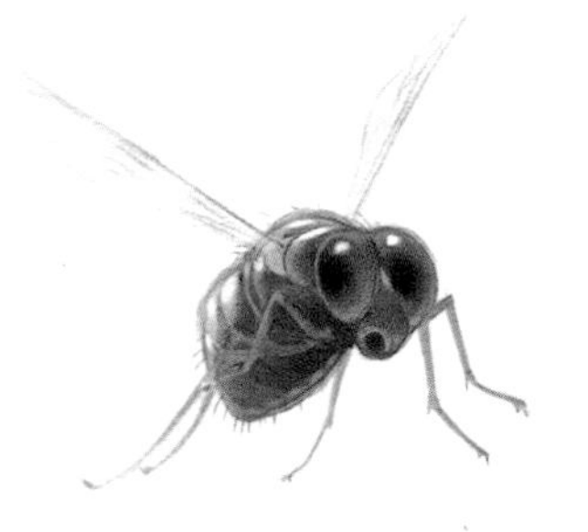

And if you see
a crabby
crocodile ...

say,

“HELP!”

Ahhh!
Shhh!
Peee-ew!
Yuck!
Oooh!
Yikes!
Ouch!
Wow!
Eeek!
Help!